The Riches of
Oseola McCarty

Evelyn Coleman

THE RICHES OF Oseola McCarty

Evelyn Coleman

ILLUSTRATED BY Daniel Minter

Albert Whitman & Company

Morton Grove, Illinois

Also by Evelyn Coleman: *White Socks Only* and *To Be a Drum*.

Library of Congress Cataloging-in-Publication Data
Coleman, Evelyn, 1948-
The riches of Oseola McCarty / by Evelyn Coleman;
illustrated by Daniel Minter.
p. cm.
Summary: A brief biography of Oseola McCarty, a hard-working washerwoman who, without a formal education herself, donated a portion of her life savings to the University of Southern Mississippi to endow a scholarship fund for needy students.
ISBN: 0-8075-6961-5
1. McCarty, Oseola—Juvenile literature.
2. Afro-American women—Mississippi—Hattiesburg—Biography—Juvenile literature.
3. Women benefactors—Mississippi—Hattiesburg—Biography—Juvenile literature.
4. University of Southern Mississippi—Benefactors—Biography—Juvenile literature.
5. Scholarships—Mississippi—Hattiesburg—History—20th century—Juvenile literature.
6. Laundresses—Mississippi—Hattiesburg—Biography—Juvenile literature.
7. Hattiesburg (Miss.)—Biography—Juvenile literature.
[1. McCarty, Oseola. 2. Philanthropists. 3. Laundresses.
4. Afro-Americans—Biography. 5. Women—Biography.]
I. Minter, Daniel, ill. II. Title.
F349.H36M383 1998 976.2'18 [b]—DC21 98-11570 CIP AC

Published in 1998 by Albert Whitman & Company, 6340 Oakton Street, Morton Grove, Illinois, 60053-2723. Published simultaneously in Canada by General Publishing, Limited, Toronto.
Printed in the United States of America.
10 9 8 7 6 5 4 3

The illustrations are block prints.
The design is by Scott Piehl.

To Lillie McLaurin, a woman I wished I could also write about.
Ms. McLaurin was the first black woman to own a newsstand
in the South. She trained and groomed paper boys and girls who
grew up respecting the ethic of work. She has dedicated her life
to the community of Hattiesburg.

And to Dr. Sandra Gibbs, Dr. Pauletta Bracy, Sylvia Sprinkle Hamlin,
Susie Wilde, Barbara Bryant, Dr. Pamela Baron, and others who
care deeply about my work for children. —E. C.

To Amanda, Shanique, Jessica, and Kira. —D. M.

HOLY BIBLE

CHAPTER ONE

Early each morning, when the sun burst through the clouds and the moon faded from sight, five-year-old Ola McCarty hopped from her bed. Her name was Oseola, but her family always called her Ola. It was 1913, and Ola had just moved to the bustling sawmill town of Hattiesburg, Mississippi, to live with her grandmother Julia and her aunt Evelyn. They lived together in a rented six-room house which later would become their own home.

Ola loved living in this new place. Hattiesburg was the headquarters for the Mississippi Central Railroad. It had three large lumber mills, many stores, and even trolley cars. It was very different from D'Lo, the nearby small town where Ola had lived. Her mother, Lucy, remained in D'Lo with Ola's stepfather, who worked in the turpentine industry.

Ola dressed quickly and raced outside. It was time for work. She fed the chickens and gathered wood for the times the fire under the wash pot might burn too low. Then she fed the hogs.

Now it was time to play. Ola made mud cakes, chased her Red Durrah Jersey pig, and flew her homemade kite with Pout, her little dog. On sunny days, she made herself dolls from roots and long blades of grass. Ola liked to play, but what she really wanted to do was work alongside her grandmother.

Sometimes Ola stopped playing to watch her grandmother drop clothes into the big black iron wash pot. She watched the fire spark underneath it. The clothes boiled and bubbled inside this pot that had been in the family for many years.

Next, her grandmother took a long stick and moved the steaming clothes from the wash pot to metal washtubs. Ola wasn't big enough to get up to the tubs, but one day her grandmother set her on top of a box so that her hands could reach inside. Ola was so excited! She swished her hands in the warm, soapy water until she grabbed one of her own slips. She scrubbed the slip up and down along the ridges of the metal scrubboard. When she was sure it was clean, she dipped the slip into the first tub of clear water and swirled it round and round. She squeezed out some of the water and dunked the slip into the second rinsing tub. Then she wrung it out as tightly

as her small hands would allow. Now the slip was ready to hang on the line to dry. Ola felt great satisfaction at having completed a grownup task.

Her grandmother also made soap in the wash pot. Ola learned how from watching her. First her grandmother scooped in big spoonfuls of leftover cooking grease. She waited until the grease boiled and then sprinkled crystals of Red Devil lye over it. She added water and boiled the mixture, stirring sometimes, until it was smooth and thick. She poured the soap into a large square pan and let it cool. Then she cut it into bars and left it to dry. By the next morning, her lye soap was ready. Ola's grandmother believed you had to do this work in the full of the moon or the soap would not turn out right.

CHAPTER TWO

Not long after Ola arrived in Hattiesburg, her mother and stepfather moved to Chicago, Illinois, leaving Ola behind. They were hard workers, and like many Southern African-Americans in those years, they thought they could find better job opportunities in the North. Ola's grandmother was glad to keep her. She thought the North was no place for her granddaughter to be left with strangers while her parents worked.

Oseola McCarty's whole family believed in hard work. Her grandmother worked six days a week at home washing and ironing clothes for white people, and young Ola helped whenever she could. Her aunt Evelyn cooked for white families and returned home in the evenings to help in the family wash business.

The South at this time was governed by "Jim Crow" laws. These laws, designed by whites, discriminated against black people. Black people were not allowed equal access to jobs, education, or even restaurants and public bathrooms, and were often denied their voting rights. Because of these laws, black people held only the most menial jobs. Many black men in Hattiesburg worked as laborers in the mills, but black women worked in the homes of white people. Even very poor white families could afford the low wages paid to black women.

Some black women lived in the houses of white

families and only saw their own children in their precious time off. Other women lived at home but did "day work" for white people. Often the trip to and from their day job, plus doing the work once there, took up most of the day and evening. There were few hours left for the women to tend to their own families. Because she worked at home, Ola's grandmother could spend time with Ola. Washing other people's clothes was a way that she and other Southern black women could earn money in their own homes.

In those days, very few people had washing machines. Each week, clothes had to be scrubbed, rinsed, wrung out, starched, hung to dry, and ironed by hand. Laundering clothes was exhausting and took many hours. People who could afford it hired others to do the backbreaking work.

Ola began attending the Eureka Elementary

School when she was six. The school had only black students because laws in the South did not allow black children and white children to attend together.

Ola was very shy, and she didn't make many friends. When she was in the sixth grade, her aunt Evelyn became very ill. Ola had to quit school to care for her aunt while her grandmother washed and ironed to support the family.

The following fall, Ola's aunt got better and was able to work again. Ola returned to school, but all her classmates had gone on to another grade. She was very unhappy at school, and also felt she was still needed at home. At that time, children often left school to help their families make a decent living, and Ola was allowed to drop out. She helped her grandmother wash and made trips to the customers' houses, picking up the bundles of soiled laundry and returning the cleaned, pressed clothes. She became

a vital part of her family's washing business.

Ola and her grandmother began their morning chores around seven and worked until eleven at night, taking short breaks to fix and eat lunch and dinner. They'd scrub and boil the clothes, wring them out with their bare hands, and hang them on the wire line with wooden clothespins. Then they'd start the washing process over again. After the clothes dried, they'd take them down and fold them.

Sometimes, in the bitterness of winter, they hung the clothes on their screened-in back porch. Eventually they bought a hand wringer. Ola would tuck the corner of a sheet between the wringer's two rollers. Then she'd wind the handle until the sheet slipped through the rollers, squeezing all the water out in the process. Now the clothes would be almost dry before they went on the lines.

Ola loved seeing the white sheets blowing in the

wind and the table linens whipping wildly through the air. She pretended they were sails on a great ship or angels flying down from the sky.

Ola and her grandmother washed from Monday through Saturday from sunup to sundown. They would iron the clothes each night except Sunday. Because clothes were made from natural fibers like cotton, they were very wrinkled after drying, and there were no steam irons—only flat, heavy metal irons that had to be heated on the stove. Ola, her grandmother, and her aunt Evelyn would stand, ironing boards lined side by side, singing and talking by lamplight until the wee hours of the night. When it was time to go to bed, they bid each other good-night and slept soundly till morning, when they began their work again.

These were the rituals the McCarty women loved—the rituals of work.

CHAPTER THREE

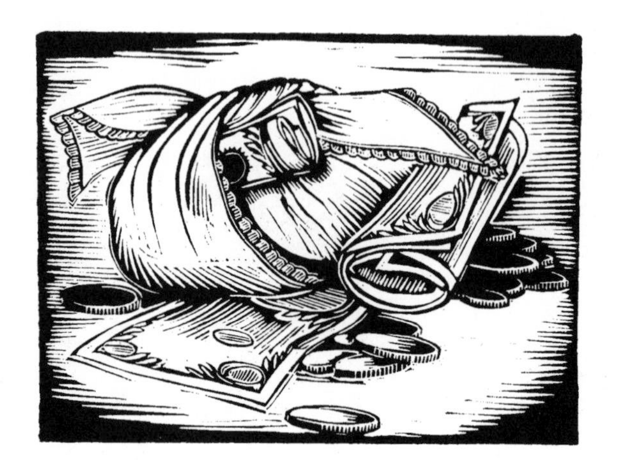

Ola missed school, but she enjoyed staying home with her family. Soon her grandmother began to pay her for her help. The McCartys did not make a lot of money. From about 1920 to 1935, black washerwomen in Mississippi made from 50¢ to $1.50 a bundle. A bundle was determined by how many clothes could be tied inside a sheet. Some people could put a lot of clothes into that $1.50 bundle.

Between them, Ola and her grandmother could wash five or six medium-sized bundles in a day. This was at a time when a pound of coffee cost 50¢, a loaf of bread was 12¢, and a basic pair of shoes was $11.50. The McCartys' low wages remained about the same even as prices rose.

Times were hard, but Ola's family focused on the work they had to do. Ola knew that even though they didn't make much money, her grandmother managed to save. She stuffed bills and coins, tied inside lace handkerchiefs, under the mattress. Sometimes she put money in a tin can in the cupboard or under the linens in the wardrobe. By saving for a rainy day, Ola's grandmother was always able to honor her debts. Ola wanted to be the same way when she grew up.

Ola knew how important saving was to her family. Her uncle John, who worked at the Hercules Powder

Company in Hattiesburg, had saved enough money to purchase the house they lived in. Then he bought another house for himself and his wife and children.

When she was about eleven, Ola began saving her money for candy. She hid it in the one spot none of the grownups ever touched—inside her hand-me-down doll carriage underneath the little satin mattress. Saving would become an important part of Ola's life.

As a teenager, Ola realized that one day her grandmother would get old and be unable to work. She decided she would save her money for that day. Ola always went to town to pay the family's bills. On one of those trips, she believed God inspired her to put money in a bank. No one in her family had ever put money in a bank before.

All alone, she walked into a Hattiesburg bank and opened her first account. On her return home, she

proudly showed her grandmother and aunt her first deposit stamped inside her passbook.

Ola's grandmother and aunt were happy that the child they'd raised had grown into a responsible young woman. Soon they sent their money with Ola to be deposited into their own accounts.

Church was important to Ola and her grandmother. Every Sunday they journeyed on foot to the Friendship Baptist Church a few miles away for Sunday school. Church services were held on the first Sunday of the month. At church, Ola's spirit rejoiced and was revived as the lively sounds of music and gospel singing filled the air. The quiet closing hymn left her heart peaceful and serene. At home in the late evenings, Ola and her grandmother read the Bible aloud together.

When Ola was thirteen, she dressed in a white gown, white stockings, and white shoes, and walked

with her grandmother and her congregation from the church to a pond. The minister and a deacon held Ola gently and dipped her head under the cool water. Ola was baptized that day. It was a moment she would never forget.

When Ola was about twenty, her mother returned and joined the other women in their business. By then Ola's stepfather had been killed in a flood. Ola's uncle Albert built the women a wash house in the backyard so they could wash in rainy weather. The McCarty women were counted among the best washerwomen in Hattiesburg. Year after year, they washed and ironed, and they took great pride in their work.

Once Ola's grandmother became ill. Ola went to the hospital to be with her. She saw nurses in their crisp white uniforms and caps and admired the beautiful outfits. She thought the nurses looked like angels. From that day on, Ola wanted to become a nurse. But she didn't have enough education. It was the first time she regretted not having gone back to school.

But Ola did not let a lack of education keep her from learning to do other things. In the 1940s, she studied with a local beautician until she received her license as a hairdresser. She began doing hair at home for people in the neighborhood. And she continued to work in the family wash business.

Ola's grandmother died in 1944, when Ola was thirty-six. Before her death, Ola took care of her, sleeping in a cot next to her bed so she wouldn't have to call out if she needed anything. Ola was the best nurse her grandmother could have had.

CHAPTER FOUR

Ola both fixed hair and washed clothes for eighteen years. She continued to save even after her grandmother died, adding to her savings money that her grandmother left her. Now she saved so she could care for her mother and aunt if they became ill. Every month, she traveled to town to bank her money. No matter how tough times were, Ola never once took money out of her account.

As her grandmother and aunt grew older, Ola had taken on more of the work. Her reputation as a washerwoman grew to legendary proportions. One day during World War II, a truck from nearby Camp Shelby rumbled loud as thunder up the road, bringing Ola army uniforms to wash and iron. The officer told Ola the army was dissatisfied with commercial laundries and wanted her to do their uniforms. Ola was proud to wash and iron for her country. Still using the black iron pot, she laundered the soldiers' shirts, pants, and underwear.

By the 1950s, many people had washing machines and driers. Ola stopped washing clothes for most of her clients though she continued to iron. She bought her own washing machine but was not happy with the way it cleaned her clothes. She gave the machine to a cousin.

Ola's mother died in 1964 and her aunt in 1967. Ola

continued the business on her own. She had washed and ironed for almost fifty years—through World War I, the Great Depression of the 1930s, World War II, and the civil-rights movement of the 1960s. Now some of her customers were black. Because of the civil-rights movement, black people could get a better education and could work in jobs previously denied them. With higher incomes, they could afford to pay someone to do their ironing. Ola was proud to be able to work for her own people. She realized that African-Americans had fought and won a long battle for justice.

Ola was making more money also—$5 a bundle after 1960 and even $10 to $20 a bundle later on.

The years went by. Ola continued to iron for the people of Hattiesburg until she was eighty-seven. One day, she fainted while she was ironing. Her doctor recommended that she stop work for good.

Ola did not want to retire. Her work had brought her pleasure and fulfillment. "If I ever get able to, I want to go back to work," she once said.

Ola had not married and had no children. She was often sad that she was alone, but she sought refuge in what she knew best: her relationship with God.

Her grandmother had taught her to rely on the company of God. Ola spent many hours each day reading her Bible.

Ola remained in her six-room house, which her uncle John had left her in the late nineteen-forties. She lived very modestly, yet she had all the things she wanted. Because she had no car, she walked everywhere and even pushed a cart to the Big Star supermarket, a mile away. She cared for her plants and flowers. She did not talk much because there were few people to talk to since the death of her close-knit family. She was happy with her life, but she had one

major regret: she had not finished her education.

All her long life, Ola had saved her money. Month after month, her savings had grown. Money her grandmother, mother, and aunt had left her had been added to the savings account. Now, Ola had a lot of money.

She was growing old, and someday she would die. To whom would she give all this money?

Ola had spent many days at her home, washing and ironing, and she had watched children go back and forth to school, generation after generation. They had the chance she never had. She thought about leaving her money to the public school, then decided it was more important to help people go on to college. She chose the University of Southern Mississippi because it was in Hattiesburg.

Ola wanted young people to understand that two things could enrich their lives. The first was a job well done. The second was education—what she wished so much to have had.

So in July 1995, eighty-seven-year-old Ola established a trust fund at a local bank. This made sure that at least $150,000 would go to the University of Southern Mississippi for the Oseola McCarty Scholarship. Each year, some of her money would help a high-school graduate from Mississippi go to college. Her banker had already set aside money so that Ola herself would always be taken care of.

Ola made her first visit to a college campus on August 29, 1995. There, at the University of Southern Mississippi, one thousand teachers and staff members stood and cheered as she walked in. In September the Hattiesburg community celebrated Oseola McCarty Day to honor Ola's generosity.

Ola became famous. People were amazed that a washerwoman could save so much money and then give a large amount away. President Bill Clinton awarded her the Presidential Citizens Medal, the nation's second-highest civilian honor. Wearing a new dress, Ola traveled to the White House to receive the medal.

Until now, Ola had been outside Mississippi only once. In the next three years, she took seventy-four trips to thirty-four cities across the country to receive awards, and she appeared on national television. She was also featured in many magazines and newspapers. A book, *Simple Wisdom for Rich Living*, was written about her life and thoughts, and she was honored by several universities. Before the 1996 Olympics, she was chosen to carry the Olympic torch for a few blocks in her home state—wearing shorts for the first time! Ted Turner, a wealthy businessman, said her unselfishness had inspired his gift of $1 billion to the United Nations. But the

tribute that meant most to Ola was an honorary nursing degree from the Baptist Memorial Hospital School of Nursing in Memphis, Tennessee.

The first Oseola McCarty Scholarship went to Stephanie Bullock in 1995. Stephanie was an African-American high-school honors graduate from Hattiesburg. She became Ola's goddaughter.

After that the scholarship grew and grew. In the fall of 1995, local businessmen and women, many having worn shirts or dresses washed and ironed by Ola's hands, set about to match her gift—and did. Moved by her generosity, more than six hundred people from thirty states also gave money to Ola's scholarship. The fund quickly reached almost $380,000, and six needy students soon had their tuition paid. The first Oseola McCarty scholar graduated in 1998.

Ola continued to live simply. She used her new

window air conditioner only when she had company. She shopped carefully. And she still saved her money.

In the summer of 1997, when asked what she would say to children for them to remember always, she responded: "If you do work that you're proud of, you will always have self-esteem. There is nothing more important than getting your education. And you should always do the work that you love."

NOTE

Ola still lives a simple life, only now it's changed. Her days are filled with hugs from people who love and care. While I visited with Ola, Stephanie Bullock, the first scholarship recipient, stopped by to introduce a friend. And when we walked through the mall together, Ola waved and smiled at her admirers. A young store clerk recognized her and rushed over to wish her luck. A couple from India stopped to invite her to their store for free ice cream. People from all ethnic groups and all walks of life greeted her as we traveled through Hattiesburg.

On Sunday we worshipped at her church, where she was asked to say a few words to the high-school graduates. She urged them "to get all the education you can," and added, "I wish I could have gotten more education."

I hope this book will show that education is a wonderful opportunity that cannot be taken for granted; that through savings, even small amounts of money can grow to large sums; and that work, no matter how ordinary, can be a source of great pride and satisfaction.

We tell children that without hard work and sacrifice, they will never amount to much. Yet, we're in a world that hardly ever celebrates the people who are up at the crack of dawn each day, doing hard, often exhausting work. Instead, we offer our applause and honors to people known as "celebrities." The day laborer, the construction worker, the service station attendant, the grocery store clerk—even the teacher—seldom get more than a nod and a thank you.

Nevertheless, it is these unsung folk who make our world a better place to live in.

I wanted to write about Oseola McCarty, but not because she gave the university money, or even because she saved so much money. I wanted to write about her because her life exemplifies these truths: all work has value, and it is important to discover work you can love.

It is when we teach children that the only reason we work is to have money that we end up with people doing less than honorable things. We end up with harmful jobs that hurt our community and our world.

We must teach our children to work not for fame and fortune, but because work offers fulfillment and dignity. In work we find who we are, and offer our talents back to the world.

My father always told me there was great honor in all work. It is not helpful to believe that some jobs are more important than others. Anyone doing a fair, honest day's work deserves our respect.

When children read this book, I hope they learn the valuable lessons that Oseola McCarty's life teaches:

Save for a rainy day.

Educate yourself so that you may do any job you decide to pursue.

Find what you love to do and let that be your work.

No matter what your work is, do it as well as you can.

Give to others, for it can bring you great joy.

It is never too late to achieve your dreams or goals, no matter your age, race, gender, or present life situation.

—Evelyn Coleman

YOUR OWN SAVINGS PLAN

How old do I have to be to open my own account?

Your parent or guardian can open an account for you as early as the day you're born.

Can it be in my name alone?

Usually a child's name and a parent or guardian's name are on the account.

How do I open my account?

With your parent or guardian, go to a bank and ask to open an account for minors (in most states, people under eighteen) or a special savings account for kids.

What types of savings plans are available?

Most banks offer kids' savings accounts or saving clubs.

What is the least amount I need to deposit to open an account?

The minimum deposit varies by bank. Often it's as little as $5.00. Your banker can explain the account to you.

Can I take out my money by myself?

It depends on the account. Bank laws for minors vary by state, but usually the adult whose name is on your account must sign when you take the money out. But remember, Ms. McCarty was able to save so much because she didn't take any money out once she put it in.

How do I know which bank to choose?

Choose a bank convenient to your home or in a place where you will be often. For instance, some supermarkets have banks inside.

Compare service charges (charges a bank makes for allowing you to have an account) and interest rates (interest is the amount of money that the bank will add to your money over time).

How is interest determined?

You can find calculators that will help you figure out how much interest your savings will get on the Internet at www.aba.com or www.kidsbank.com, or you can ask your banker.

How do I set savings goals?

Decide how much money you would like to save each week or month and use the interest calculator to determine how much it will grow. If you deposit $10.00 a month at 4.5 percent interest and don't take any money out, in a year you will have $122.51.

Sometimes you'll want to use your money to buy yourself or someone else a special present. But the trick is to make savings a lifelong habit—then it really pays off. If you kept putting your $10.00 a month in the bank and never took any of it out for fifty years, you'd have put in only $6,000.00 but you'd have $22,527.72 in your account! (Ms. McCarty saved money for about eighty years.) Of course, the more money you put in, the faster your savings will grow.

Think about saving your money in a piggy bank until you build up to the amount you want to deposit weekly or monthly. Ms. McCarty first saved her money in her doll carriage.

And remember, if you get money for your birthday, holidays, an allowance, or a job, always put a portion of it into your savings account.

ACKNOWLEDGMENTS

My deepest gratitude goes to Ms. Oseola McCarty for welcoming me in her home and sharing her life story with the world.

I could not have done this book without Abby Levine, who did an incredible editing job and coached and held my hand though this process. Thanks also to Kathy Tucker and Joe Boyd of Albert Whitman & Company, who always support my work. And Scott Piehl, who continually amazes me with his vision. And, of course, thanks to Daniel Minter, whose great art always takes my words to another level.

Thanks also to:

William E. "Bud" Kirkpatrick and J. T. Tisdale of the University of Southern Mississippi's Public Relations Department, who graciously offered valuable assistance.

Jewel Tucker, the woman closest to Ms. McCarty, for answering my endless questions.

Paul Laughlin, vice-president and trust officer of the Trustmark National Bank, Hattiesburg, a long-time friend and financial adviser to Ms. McCarty. He also provided the sample bankbook page on p. 45.

Dr. Bobs M. Tusa, archivist, and Yvonne Arnold, archives specialist, at the University of Southern Mississippi, who helped me find important resources. They also let me see and touch the iron pot Ms. McCarty washed in all those years.

The Red Bailey family, with their wonderful historic bed and breakfast. If you're in Hattiesburg, it's a great place to stay.

My mother, Annie S. Coleman, who remembered how my grandmother made soap.

Kathryn Kelly and Hans

Johnson of the American Bankers Association Education Foundation, who helped with banking questions.

Raylawni Branch, one of the first black graduates of the University of Southern Mississippi, who gave me vital information regarding the people of Hattiesburg.

Eliza McCann, Ms. McCarty's neighbor and relative by marriage, for giving me insight into the life of Ms. McCarty and the Hattiesburg community.

Abraham Pack, who has his own wonderful story of how through hard work he became the owner of the Liberty Cab Company of Hattiesburg. Thanks for introducing me to the people of Hattiesburg, who helped me understand the African-American perspective of this story.

Sandra Newell and Sandra Shelton, dispatchers for the Liberty Cab Company, who assisted me each time I phoned.

Billy Scaggs, Fulton County, Georgia, extension agent, who gave me the current name for the Red Durrah Jersey pig and informed me the pig is popular on farms today.

Sherri Bowers, reference librarian at the Fulton County Public Library, Atlanta, for answering questions about different periods in our history.

Chris Snell, director of the Fayette County, Georgia, Public Library and a close friend, for her assistance.

Tera W. Hunter for writing the informative book *To 'Joy My Freedom: Southern Black Women's Lives and Labors after the Civil War*, and for answering my questions over the telephone.

OTHER RESOURCES

Federal Writers' Project of the Works Progress Administration, *Mississippi: The WPA Guide to the Magnolia State*. New York: Viking Press, 1938. Reprint. Jackson, Miss.: University Press of Mississippi, 1988.

Hallie Brooks, interview by Bernard E. West, February 27, 1979, Living Atlanta Collection, Atlanta Historical Society, Atlanta, Georgia.

N. R. Burger, interview by R. Wayne Pyle, vol. 356, 1982; Lillie Burney, interview by Dr. Orley B. Caudill, vol. 292, 1975; Pete Peters, interview by Dr. Orley B. Caudill, vol. 550, 1974; all in the Mississippi Oral History Program of the University of Southern Mississippi, Hattiesburg, Mississippi.

The Hattiesburg American, articles from 1918, 1934, 1948, 1964, 1966.

The Hattiesburg Daily News, articles from 1913-1914.

The American Bankers Association sponsors an annual National Teach Children to Save Day. To find out the date and more information, phone Kathryn Kelly at 1-800-338-0626, or write the ABA Education Foundation, 1120 Connecticut Avenue N.W., Washington, D.C. 20036. You may visit their website at www.aba.com/aba/Edu_Foun, or e-mail Ms. Kelly at EduFoun@aba.com.The American Bankers Association Education Foundation helped to answer the savings-related questions on pp. 44–45.